D0876598

Kathryn Apel is a born-and-bred farm girl who's scared of cows. She lives with her husband and two sons among the gum trees, cattle and kangaroos on a Queensland grazing property. *Too Many Friends* is Kathryn's fifth book, and third verse novel following the release of *On Track* (2015) and *Bully on the Bus* (2014) to much acclaim. Kathryn loves pumping poetry because she can flex her muscles across other genres, to bend (and break) writing rules. Kathryn teaches part-time and shares her passion for words at schools and festivals.

www.katswhiskers.wordpress.com

DEC - - 2019

Also by Kathryn Apel
Bully on the Bus
On Track

DEC - - 2019

TOO MANY FRIENDS

KATHRYN APEL

UQP

WILLIAMSBURG REGIONAL LIBRARY
7770 CROAKER ROAD
WILLIAMSBURG, VA 23188

First published 2017 by University of Queensland Press
PO Box 6042, St Lucia, Queensland 4067 Australia

www.uqp.com.au
uqp@uqp.uq.edu.au

© Kathryn Apel 2017

This book is copyright. Except for private study, research, criticism or reviews, as permitted under the Copyright Act, no part of this book may be reproduced, stored in a retrieval system, or transmitted in any form or by any means without prior written permission. Enquiries should be made to the publisher.

Cover design and illustration by Jo Hunt
Typeset in 13/19 pt Adobe Garamond by Post Pre-press Group, Brisbane
Printed in Australia by McPherson's Printing Group, Melbourne

Queensland
Government

The University of Queensland Press
is supported by the Queensland
Government through Arts Queensland.

Australia
Council
for the Arts
Australian Government

The University of Queensland Press
is assisted by the Australian Government
through the Australia Council, its arts
funding and advisory body.

Cataloguing-in-Publication Data
National Library of Australia
http://catalogue.nla.gov.au

Apel, Kathryn, author.
Too Many Friends / Kathryn Apel.

ISBN 978 0 7022 5976 0 (pbk)
ISBN 978 0 7022 5946 3 (pdf)
ISBN 978 0 7022 5947 0 (epub)
ISBN 978 0 7022 5948 7 (kindle)

For primary school age.

Friendship – Juvenile fiction.
Students – Juvenile fiction.
Novels in verse.

A823.4

University of Queensland Press uses papers that are natural, renewable and recyclable products made from wood grown in sustainable forests. The logging and manufacturing processes conform to the environmental regulations of the country of origin.

WILLIAMSBURG REGIONAL LIBRARY
7770 CROAKER ROAD
WILLIAMSBURG, VA 23188

To my sister.
You are a good friend because you listen, love and laugh.

CONTENTS

FRIENDS
WITH
EVERYONE

Pieces of Me

At school
I have lots of friends.

I have so many friends that
sometimes I
don't know
              who
                 to
                    play
                       with.

'What are we
going to play
today, Tahnee?'

    'Tahnee,
    come to the library
    with us!'

        'Do you want to
        skip with us,
        Tahnee?'

'Tahnee's
playing horses
with us today!'

Sometimes I feel like
all my friends are
                    reaching,
         grabbing,
                    snatching,
stretching,
                         squashing,
      squeezing,
                         pulling,
until I think that I might
         CRACK!

3

Sharing

I like my friends.
I like to be with ALL of my friends.
But sometimes my friends
aren't friendly with
each other.

I can't play all their games
all the time,
and sometimes
what I want to play
isn't what *all* my friends
want to play.
Even though I tell them
they're still my friends
(because they are –
I like them *all*
even when I'm *not* with them),
I still can't
make *all* my friends happy
ALL the time …

                        And that
                        makes me
                            sad.

My Friends

Why can't we all just be friends?

Just because I'm playing with
  Pia,
doesn't mean I don't like
   Roxie.
And just because I have fun with
     Ashton,
doesn't mean I don't like being with
      Heidi.
And even though he can be annoying, I still like
       Michael.
And sometimes I want to be by
       myself.
But that doesn't mean I don't like
       all
my friends!

I want everyone to be friends
and to be friends with everyone.

But sometimes it seems like there
isn't
enough
of me to be a
good friend to

anyone.

Friendly Family

My dad says,
'Everybody
needs friends.'

My big sister, Ella, says,
'You can't have
too many friends.'

'*Good* friends
can be hard to find,'
Mum says.

I say,
'I want to be a
good friend,
so I try to be friendly
                    to everyone.'

I like friends.

I Don't Eat My Friends!

The kids
in my class
are like a jumbo pack of
assorted party lollies –
they're all different,
but I like them
                all.

(I don't *eat* my friends!)

Some kids
talk a lot;
others
tell funny jokes.
Some kids
ask questions
and listen lots;
others
ask questions
and don't listen *at all*.
Some kids are bossy
(sometimes too bossy!);
others like
to be told

what to do –
want you to do it
        for them.
Some kids are quiet
and always there;
others are quiet
and always alone.

All my classmates are different,

but that's the best thing
about
        friends …
                and lollies.

TEAMWORK

Everybody's Darling

Miss Darling is
my teacher.
She smiles a lot
and wears colourful clothes
with spots and stripes
and swirly patterns,
and bright, floppy flowers in her
curly, brown hair.

My sister, Ella, says
everybody
likes Miss Darling
because Miss Darling likes
everybody.

Ella says
some teachers don't really want
to be at school –
says they grumble and sigh
and sit at their desks
calling out instructions,
watching the clock
tick down
to home time.

But Miss Darling
                     smiles
as she
moves around the room
like sunshine
       chasing rainbows.

Miss Darling makes school
exciting!

Made For Fun

We're working in groups
in Science and in Technology,
to test
and make
toys.

In Science
we have to find out
what makes different toys
move –
      a push,
          or a pull.

Miss Darling calls it
force and motion:
a force is needed
to make them move.

In Technology
we have to
design and make
our own
toy
using recycled objects.

'That's stupid,' says Kody.
'Who wants to play with
a pile of rubbish?'

A cloud flickers over
Miss Darling's face.

Kody complains about everything!

'I think it sounds fun,'
I say.
'I'm already thinking about
what I could make.'

Miss Darling tells us
that later in the term
her friend,
Vika,
is coming to show us
'what kids your age
in her country
make
to play with,'

Miss Darling smiles at Kody,
'using recycled materials.'

Groups Work

I love group work because
I can work
with my friends,
and that's

fun.

Sharing ideas
gets the job done
quicker and better
because
in a group we think of
almost everything –
even some things I'd never think of
                    by
                            myself.

'Listen for your name
so you'll know
which group you're in,'
Miss Darling says
as she pulls out her list.

Michael

Michael
says (loudly) he's
group leader;
that we have to do things
his way.

Michael can be
hard work,
wanting to do things
his way
        all
            the
               time.

He gets in a miff
if anyone suggests
        something
        different,
doesn't always listen
when other people have

better ideas,

or pretends they were
his ideas all along.

Some kids
are happy for Michael
to always do it Michael's way.

But some kids

are not.

Roxanne

Roxie
doesn't like
being told what to do,
                              or what not to do;
she likes to jump in
and take charge
and DO
the fun stuff.

Roxie doesn't like
watching …
     waiting …
          wishing …
               wasting.

She's like a wind-up toy
coiled too tight,
fit to bust!

Sometimes
I think Roxie's red hair
is a spark –
ready to flare into a whole

bushfire
of trouble.

I wonder
what Miss Darling
was thinking
putting Roxie
and Michael
together.

I worry
there'll be arguments
no matter what
I do.

I worry
we won't get
the job done.

I worry.

I don't like it
when my friends
don't get
along.

Ashton

Ashton
is a joker –
he pulls faces behind
Michael's back
as Michael drones on

and on

and on,

even though
Miss Darling just told us *all*
what to do,
so we don't need
Michael to tell us *at all*!

Ashton
has so much mischief inside
that even when Michael
says things he probably shouldn't,
like, 'Why do I get stuck
with Ashton
and Roxanne?',
Ashton doesn't get grumpy
or angry (like Roxie),
he just rolls his eyes

and pulls a face
(that Michael doesn't see)
so that even Roxie
fizzes with laughter –
when before
she was winding up
to
snap, snap, snap, snap, snap, snap,
SNAP!

We giggle
(but not Michael)

until I see
Miss Darling
watching us,
a frown creasing her forehead.

'Miss Darling is watching,'
I whisper.

And Ashton appears as busy as anyone!

Sara

Sara
will record our results.

Michael says
that's best
because Sara's good at spelling,
keeps her writing neat
and organised – and she doesn't

lose things
(like Ashton),

or get
distracted
(like Roxanne).

That's what Michael says.

I think Michael is right
and Sara will be
a good note-taker,

but Michael should
think more
before he talks.

Roxie says,
'Recording results is boring!
I'm glad that's not my job.'

Sara says she'll
pop our work sheets
and notes
in the special
shimmery-swirly
aqua-blue
display book
that she keeps
in her tidy tray
for important things.

Ashton says, 'Great idea, Sara!'

Michael says, 'Humph.'

Tahnee (That's Me!)

Michael says I can be
the group's artist.

I'll draw and label
the diagrams
each time we do
an experiment.

Sometimes I'll have to draw
what others in our group
are thinking,

and that could be tricky.

Are you thinking what I'm drawing?

But I can't wait to get started.

A NEW
FRIEND

Push ... or Pull?

Before we can
test any toys,
Miss Darling says
we have to organise
pictures of toys into
categories
to predict if
the force that moves them
is a push   or pull.

'You need to keep
all of your group's work sheets
and hand them in
at the end of the unit
as part of your assessment,'
Miss Darling says.

Michael looks at Sara,
who smiles
and nods,
and I know our work sheets
will be safe in Sara's
shimmery-swirly
display book.

'Work together as a group,
and watch out for

                    t
                    r
        q u e s t i o n s,'
                    c
                    k

Miss Darling says.

29

Lucy

Even though Lucy
is taller than Pia,
shorter than Roxie,
and about the same height
as Heidi and me,
with blonde hair
like mine
and blue eyes
like Heidi's,
she is not
like me,
or my other
friends.

Lucy is new
to Year 2.

She came
in the middle of the term,
and even though
she's been in our class
for three weeks,

Lucy still doesn't seem
to have
any
friends.

'I don't think she
brushes her hair,'
Roxie hisses as we walk past Lucy
on our way
to lunch.

We sit down
on our normal seat,
where we can see
right across
the eating area.

All around us
kids are warbling
like magpies,
carolling their stories
over the chorus of other voices,
swooping and diving
into the chattering frenzy,

straining to hear
everything everyone says ...

But Lucy
is
silent
and
alone.

No Friends

I gather my rubbish,
skip across to
the bin, then
take a sip of water
at the bubblers
and skip back towards
my friends,
passing Lucy
on the way.

I smile,
but Lucy's too busy
looking at the hole in the toe
of her shoe
to notice.

I stop.

'Why are you sitting
all by yourself?' I ask.

Lucy shrugs,
peers closer at her shoe.

'Why don't you come

and sit with us?
There's lots of room,
and it's much nicer
when you're with friends.'

'I don't have any friends,' Lucy says.

The bell rings
for playtime, and
Heidi, Pia and Roxie come
rushing over.

'Come on, Tahnee,' Roxie cries.
'Let's go to the rainforest
before the Year 3 boys get there.'

Lucy starts to gather her
lunch gear together.

'Do you want to come
to the rainforest with us?'
I ask.

Lucy pauses,
looks at me,
looks at Roxie,
Heidi and Pia,

then looks away again.

She picks up her lunch box
and walks off.

'She wouldn't be any fun anyway,'
Roxie says loudly,
leading the way to the rainforest.
'She stinks.'

'Roxie!' I gasp. 'That's mean.'

'Would you like it
if someone said that
about you,
Roxie?'
Pia asks.

But Roxie isn't listening.

I remember Lucy's words.

I don't have any friends.

I try to think of ways
to show Lucy that
I'm
        her friend.

PARTY
PLANS

List of Friends

Soon it's
my seventh birthday.
Mum says
I can invite some friends
over for a
party.

That's exciting.
I've never had
a party with my
school friends.
But,
      'How many can I invite?'

Mum rolls her eyes
and laughs.
'How many friends do you have?'

I get a piece of paper,
then list
all my friends.

1. Roxie
2. Heidi
3. Pia

4. Ashton
5. Sara

.

.

.

My list keeps going
and going
until …

.

.

.

20. Lucy
21. Kody
22. Jack
23. Michael

'You can't have that many friends!'
Mum gasps.

'They're just the friends
from my class,'
I tell her.

'Even though Michael
can be annoying,
and Kody

can get grumpy,
and Jack can be a pest,
and Lucy doesn't talk much …
they're still my friends.'

Mum's mouth is open,
but her words are stuck.

'I don't want anyone to feel
                              left out,' I say,
'or sad.'

Mum nibbles at her lip,
then smiles
a wobble-worried smile
to match her wrinkle-worried eyes.

'I guess we'll just have to
make it work then,'
Mum says,

'somehow.'

Overheard

'Are you crazy?'
Dad says.
'What are we going to do with
23 kids?

I think I'm busy that Saturday –
away from home.'

I gasp.

He can't mean it!

I run outside,
letting the screen door
bang shut
behind me.

Mum and Dad
are sitting
at the outdoor setting,
but I don't wait
for them to finish
talking.

'Dad,' I burst in.
'It's my birthday party.
You *have* to be here.'

Dad starts to shake his head,
murmuring something about
an important game of golf,
but then looks
into my pleading eyes
and mumbles
to a
stop.

Mum's lips twitch.

'Of course Dad will come, Tahnee.
He wouldn't want to
miss out on
all the

fun.'

Planning a Party

I want to have a Show party –
with Show bags and games
and Show foods …

                    and fun.

Lots of fun!

All afternoon
we're busy
planning the party.

I
print the invitations,
then decorate them
with drawings,
glitter and stickers.
Fancy!

Ella
writes a list of
games we could play.

Dad
jots a 'To Do' list
to tidy the yard

and create
Sideshow Alley.

Mum
makes a list
of Show foods.

I tell Mum that
Michael can't eat
nuts,
   Heidi doesn't eat
   meat
      and Jack can't have
      red food colouring.

         'And Kody
         is allergic
         to bees,'
         I add.

Mum and Dad
both stop scratching at their lists
and look at me,
eyes wide
with alarm.

Ella shrugs.

'Trudy Tickleton
is allergic to grass seed –
and grass is everywhere!'

'I didn't think
a birthday party
could cause this much
stress,'
Mum says,
crossing honey crackles
and peanut butter boats
off her list of Show foods.

'Maybe your teacher
would like to come,'
Dad says,
'since she knows
all the kids?'

'Oooh. Yes!'
I say,
feeling bubbles of happiness
bursting inside me.

'What's one more guest?'
Mum asks.

Excuses

'They probably
won't all
be able to come,'
Mum says.

'Lots of kids
will have Saturday sport,'
Dad says.

'Everyone
loves
a party!'
Ella says.

'But it's short notice,'
Mum says.

'And they might have
other things planned,'
Dad says.

'I think they'll

> *all*

        come,'
I say.

Inviting Trouble

On Friday,
before school,
I hand out
my invitations.

I place one
on everybody's desk,
including Miss Darling's.

When I'm finished,
only one desk
is empty.

Mine.

☺

RSVP

On Monday,
everyone
is talking
about my party because
even though
Mum and Dad were sure
they wouldn't
all be able to come ...
they can!

Even Miss Darling,
who's just popping in
because
she says
she can't
resist

cake!

TOO MANY TOYS

Testing the Limit

During Science
we start testing
the effects of force
on toys.

Some toys move
when they're pushed.
Others move when they're pulled.
Something supplies
the force needed
to push
                or pull
                        them.

(And some toys
don't move at all.)

Miss Darling has brought in
heaps of toys for us to test.

Things like:
basketballs,
handballs,
cars,
trains,

frisbees,

yo-yos,

spinning tops,

roly-poly bobble animals,

plastic lawnmowers,

dolls,

wooden wagons,

playdough cutters,

marbles,

prams,

pinwheels,

shopping trolleys,

and golf carts.

There's even
a pull-along turtle!

(I wonder if the turtle's a trick.)

'Where did you GET all this?'
Ashton asks.

'You'd be surprised
what you can find in an op shop,'
Miss Darling says.

'Do we have to test them ALL?'
Jack asks.

'I'm not writing stuff about
all of them,' Kody says.

Miss Darling shakes her head.

'I didn't for a moment
think you would, Kody.
Each group has to
choose five toys to test.
And remember to record
all your results.'

Testing the Friendships

Michael says we'll test:

a train,

shopping trolley,

frisbee,

spinning top and

handball.

'I'm not testing a shopping trolley,'
Roxie says. 'I hate shopping!'

'I wanted to test the yo-yo,'
Ashton says.

'Maybe we could swap the yo-yo
and the shopping trolley,' I suggest.

Michael grumps
and says we won't have
enough variety,
so eventually we agree on:

a lawnmower,
spinning top,
yo-yo,
pinwheel and
penguin pull-toy.

And everyone is happy –

even Michael.

'That's what I said
we should test
right from the start,'
he says.

Not So Goofy

Sometimes Ashton
surprises us
because his goofy ideas
aren't so silly
after all.

'I think the yo-yo
is a trick,'
Ashton says,
'because you push
when you flick it down
and pull
when you draw it up.'

'Good thinking, Ashton,'
Sara says, writing his prediction down.

Michael frowns.

'That's only if you can
work a yo-yo,' he blusters.
'Some people
can't pull it back up again,
so then it's just a push.'

When someone has a good idea
that Michael didn't think of first,

Michael isn't happy.

Write on Time

During middle session,
Miss Darling tells us
about an exciting idea
she's had.

'We're going to work as a class
to write and edit a story
for the prep kids.'

(They read *heaps* of stories!)

'Then we're going to illustrate it,'
Miss Darling adds.

She hands out
the special 'writing' hats
we made using
          glitter,
              sparkly letters,
     foam shapes,
buttons,
     cardboard
         and curling ribbon.

'These will help you be
        creative
with your words,'
Miss Darling says
as we giggle and admire
all the different
hats.

We work together,
ideas bouncing
around the room
as Miss Darling
writes them onto
large sheets of
butcher's paper.

Sometimes
the room gets
noisy
as we share our
ideas.
Miss Darling's marker squeaks
and dashes
and our story plan starts
to take shape.

'This is easier
than writing by myself,'
Jack says.

'It's fun,' I agree.

Miss Darling checks her watch
before scanning the class.
Her eyes sparkle
and the floppy orange flower
flutters in her hair.

'We need
a character that moves
slowly …
          Lucy,
what do you think?'
Miss Darling asks.

Everyone looks at Lucy.

                    'A snail?' she asks.

    'Or a tortoise,'
Jack says.

'A sloth!'
Sara says.

Miss Darling's pen
is flying away, again.

.

.

.

Brrring!

We all jump.

'I didn't even know
it was
lunchtime,'
Kody says.

Push and Pull – Give and Take

On Wednesday
we start to test our toys
to see if they move,
as we predicted,
from a push

or a pull.

Roxanne tests the pinwheel,
and Ashton tests the yo-yo.
Michael tells us if it's a push or a pull,
then tells Sara what to write –
and me what to draw.

But Sara writes
in her words
and I draw
what I observe.

'Your group is working well today,'
Miss Darling says,
and I nod my head
(but keep working)
because *today*

she's right!

Not Working

Heidi and Pia
are working on the carpet
with Jack and Kody
(and Lucy),
and they don't look happy
about that.

'Why can't we have a turn?'
I hear Pia ask,
but I don't think that Jack or Kody
(or Lucy)
heard her.

Jack and Kody are using
far too much *force*
to propel cars
across the classroom.
(Lucy doesn't seem to notice.)

Next time I look,
Pia and Heidi have
their backs to the boys
and are busy filling out

one of the work sheets
by themselves.

Lucy is sitting beside the group
but apart from it –
not with Pia and Heidi,
or Jack and Kody.

She looks terribly

                    alone.

Heidi glances over,
her nose scrunched
and her forehead crinkled.
I try to cheer her with a smile,
but she rolls her eyes
and her lips turn down
as she nudges Pia.

Pia sighs.
'I wish we were in
your group, Tahnee.'

I wish they were, too.
It would be fun,
and they'd get more work done
in our group –

Michael would make sure of that!

'But Lucy can help you,'
I say, smiling.

Pia pinches her lips.
'Lucy never does anything!
She might as well not
be in a group.'

I cringe.

If I heard Pia,
so did Lucy.

But Lucy doesn't even flinch.

How must she feel?

'Tahnee. You're not watching,'
Roxie fusses,
pulling me back
on task
in time to see Ashton propel
the spinning top
into a dizzy dance.

I sneak a quick glance
over my shoulder as
Miss Darling moves towards
Pia and Heidi's group.

She crouches down,
drawing them all
around her.

I hope Miss Darling
can sort things out.

Not For Lunch

'Maybe Lucy
would like to sit
with us
for lunch today,'
I say
as we collect lunch boxes
from our schoolbags.
'She always seems so
alone.'

Heidi and Pia snort.

'We've tried
to be friendly,'
Pia says.

'But Lucy doesn't *want*
any friends,'
Heidi finishes.

'Just forget about her,'
Roxie says,
striding off towards
the eating area.

But I can't.

I want to be
a good friend
to Lucy.

But I don't know
how.

Editing the Teacher

On Thursday
Miss Darling puts on her bright red editor's hat.
'Now that our story
is written,' she says,
'we need to think of
better ways to say things.'

She highlights words we use lots,
like 'big', 'nice', 'bad', 'got',
and says we need to find words
that are
more 'interesting'
and 'paint a better picture'.

   Big.
      Large.
         Huge.
            Enormous.
               Immense.

And THEN ... when we finally find
the perfect word that we all really, really like and
want to use
                  over and over again ...

Miss Darling the editor says,

'Think of another word –
a better word.
You've already used

        that one.'

Miss Darling the editor is very fussy!

PARTY ON!

Countdown

'I can't wait
until your party,'
Roxie says
as we're packing our bags
at home time.

'Only one more sleep,'
I say, and I can feel
excitement shiver
my shoulders,
and jiggle down
to my toes.
                        'It's going to be

                                so

                                much

                                fun!'

'Roll up! Roll up!'
Ashton trumpets,
his newsletter *rolled up*
like a megaphone.
'It's … Show Time!'

Lucy squeezes out of
the pressing, pushing bodies,
then slips on her backpack.

'See you tomorrow, Lucy?' I call.

Lucy dips her head,
then walks
away.

I hope she comes.

It's ... Show Time!

Our front yard looks like
a festive fun park, with streamers,
                              bunting,
            balloons
and brightly coloured party favours
fluttering about
in the spring breeze.

Everything is ready:
                              pin the tail on the pony,
            photo booth,
                              mimes,
            face painting,
                              balloon car racers,
            ribbon dancing,
                              a-mazing maze,
            karaoke,
                              Twister,
            quoits,
                              skittles,
            lucky dip,
                              pass the parcel

            and food!

'There's something for everyone,'
Mum says,

> 'I hope.'

Hot dogs,
  popcorn,
    pizza,
      fairy floss,
        cupcakes,
          corn on the cob,
            slushies,
              hot chips,
                fruit salad.

But no nuts.
No red lollies.
And no honey crackles.

'Do bees even *like* honey?' I ask Ella.

Duck, Dad!

'I still don't
know why *I* have
to be the one everyone
throws wet sponges at,' Dad grumbles,
flapping around in his orange flippers,
and yellow shirt and boardies,
with bright yellow zinc
smeared over his
nose and cheeks.

'Because "Duck, Dad!"
is a good name
for a game,' I say.

'And when Kody and Jack start throwing wet
sponges,' Ella laughs, 'you'll want to *duck, Dad*!'

'I still think "Duck, *Mum*!" sounds better,' Dad says,
flicking a spray of water at Mum, as he gathers his
bucket of soggy sponges, ready for the game.

I pop Dad's special party hat on his head like a
crown; wide yellow band, bright orange
cardboard bill and large, round eyes.

Quack!

Ella, Mum
and I giggle as
Dad flap-flops flippered
feet across the lawn towards
Sideshow Alley.

'This party is not all it's *quacked*
up to be,' Dad mumbles,
but I hear the laughter
in his voice.

Reactions

Roxie: I'm first at Duck, Dad!

Michael: I can show you all how to play mimes.

Ashton: Are all these presents for *ME*?

Pia: I don't know where to start.

Jack: That maze is a-mazing! Get it?

Sara: Your dad is so funny!

Heidi: It's like we're at the Show.

Kody: I'd be embarrassed if my dad did that.

Ella: Who wants their face painted?

Lucy:

Carnival Craze

My friends rush
from game to food to activity,
try things out,
then rush on
to something new.

I try to talk to
everyone ...
make them all
welcome,
but sometimes they
flit and fly
so fast,
I just can't keep up.

Everyone is having FUN!

But is Lucy?

> She's sitting
> on a plastic chair
> beside the party food,
>   watching ...
>
> but not joining in.

'Have you had a go
at the lucky dip?'
I ask her.

Lucy shakes her head,
but doesn't move.

Pass the Parcel

Michael is grumpy
because Kody and Jack
won't play mimes
his way –
won't play with him
at all
anymore.

'I'm gonna see
how many times I can
splat Tahnee's dad,'
Kody says.
'I'm beating Jack.'

'Come and play mimes
with me, Tahnee,'
Michael says.

But Lucy is sitting
all by herself –
again –
watching,
but not joining in
with any of the games.

I think
the only one
who's spent
any time
talking with her
all afternoon is
me.

'Maybe you could ask Lucy,'
I tell Michael,
because I've just spied Heidi
hiding behind the garden shed,
not hide-and-seek hiding
but hide-and-weep hiding.

Why is Heidi upset?

'Tahnee!
You haven't even opened your
presents yet.'
Roxie grabs my arm,
and pulls me towards
the loaded table of
tinsel, ribbon and wrapping paper.

I look around,
see Heidi hiding,
   Lucy on her lonesome,
      Michael in a miff at miming
         and …

'Photo bomb!'

… popping in
and out of
      the photo booth
like a jack-in-a-box
is …

'Jack!

Why do you always have to be
      such (!) a (!) pest (!)?'
Sara says,
storming out of the photo booth
followed by Pia
and Ashton.

'That's another hit for me!'
Kody cries, as Dad

lobs the squishy sponge
back into the bucket and
Roxie tugs at my arm again.
'You'll never guess what I got you.
Open mine first!'
she says.

Sara and Pia come
running up,
grabbing their presents
and thrusting them into my hands,
so that it almost feels like
I'm the parcel,
and everyone is snatching,
grabbing,

          pushing,

    pulling,

            lobbing

        me

around the circle,
tearing at the paper
and tossing layers
away.

'Where's the birthday girl?'
Dad bellows,
galumphing across the yard
in his squeaky duck-feet flippers.

'I think it must be time to plaaaaay …

                              pass the parcel.'

Subtractions

Michael: Roxie, you're holding it too long.

Pia: I love this song!

Jack: Shake it! See if it rattles.

Ashton: I think I can guess what it is.

Heidi: I haven't unwrapped any.

Kody: It's probably something for girls.

Sara: Oooh. It's getting very small …

Roxie: Mi–chael! I am *not*.

Mum: That's right, honey. Rip the paper off.

Lucy: Oh. A yo-yo.

Consuming Worries

Jack said
Kody couldn't
beat him in a pizza-
eating competition, and
now the pizza's gone and Pia
didn't have any, and Ashton
wants to know why there's no
red lollies because they're his
favourite, and Roxie says (loudly)
it's because of Jack, who says it's
not his fault – he doesn't even
like red lollies, and Heidi isn't
hungry but Michael sure is,
and if Miss Darling doesn't
get here soon, there'll
be no food left!

But
Lucy likes
fairy floss.
Yay!

Interactions

Michael: Why won't anyone do mimes with me?

Pia: Help! I'm stuck in the maze.

Jack: Photo bomb!

Ashton: Has anyone seen Heidi?

Heidi: *Sniff*

Kody: If this was *my* party, my dad would have a *real* dunking machine.

Sara: You still haven't gone in the photo booth with me, Tahnee.

Roxie: You said you'd open *my* present first.

Dad: Come on, Lucy. *Quack!* It must be your turn.

Lucy: *Shakes her head*

Miss Darling: Am I too late for cake?

The Icing on the Cupcakes

'Oooh.
So many!'
Miss Darling says
as we gather around
my birthday cupcakes.
'How will we ever
choose!'

I giggle.
Miss Darling
sounds just like a kid.

Colourful fruit-stick lollies
fan out from a rainbow cake
in the centre of the tray.
At the end of each
lolly length,
cupcakes
(that look a bit like carriages)
are decorated with Smarties,
sprinkles and stars.
A face
is peeping over the edge
of each carriage.

'It's a Ferris wheel,' Jack says.

'And we're on it!'
Roxie cries.
'See? That one
with red hair
looks like ME!'

My friends jostle
to get closer,
then point and exclaim
when they find a cupcake
that could be
them.

'My dad knows someone
with a *real* Ferris wheel,'
Kody says loudly
to no-one in particular.

I point to the
yellow duck cupcake,
waiting in the queue
at the bottom of the Ferris wheel.
'That one's for Dad,'
I say. 'It was Ella's idea.'

'Is there one
        for everyone?'
Ashton asks.

I nod,
bouncing on my toes.
'Ella and I helped Mum
decorate them.'

'Blow out the candles and
make a wish,' Mum says.

    Dad stands ready with the
    camera. I take
    a deep breath,

        spot Lucy,
        hanging back
        behind everyone.

        WHOOOOOOOOOSH …

                *'I wish all my friends
                would all be
                friends,'*

        I whisper to myself.

Best Friends

When everyone
has left
    (even Miss Darling,
    who had cake
    and fairy floss,
    and even took a toss
    at Duck, Dad! –

    and missed),

Ella and I collapse
on the trampled grass
of our front-yard
fun park,
too exhausted
to move.

Mum
looks at all the mess
that needs
tidying up,
putting away
or binning …
then sprawls

beside
Ella
and me.

'The mess will wait,' Mum sighs.

Dad kicks off his flippers,
then flops down,
scruffy-grotty-icky-wet,
alongside us.
      'Qua-a-a-ack!'
His party hat spins sideways,
duck bill drooping around his ear.

My head and legs and
arms and feet
and tongue and brain
and smile
and
*every*thing
ache
from running after
all my friends.

'Sometimes I think I have
too many friends.'

I moan.

Dad groans – loudly.
I think that means he agrees,
although maybe it means
he wishes
I'd thought of that
before this afternoon.

Mum starts to giggle,
then gurgle,
until a rumbling belly laugh
echoes in my ears,
then burbles
out *my* mouth.
Soon we're *all*

       laughing
       uncontrollably at
       nothing.

When we have no energy
left for laughter,
Dad reaches over
and scruffs a hand
through my tangled hair.

'You sure do have lots of friends,'
he says.

'But the *best* friend I saw today

was *you*.'

TOYING
WITH
FRIENDS

Sharing and Caring

On Monday
Roxie talks about
my Show party
for show-and-tell.

'This is boring,'
Kody says.
'We all know that already.'

Heidi tells us that Bluey,
her budgie,
died
before my party.
She didn't want to come.

'I'm still sad,'
Heidi sniffs.

I feel terrible.
I wish I had known.

I show my
craft kit
from Mum and Dad
with

a rainbow of ribbons,
feathers,
felt shapes,
pom poms,
shells,
bells,
trinkets,
and sparkly glitter beads
to make into …

                         something!

'And this wind-up
chatterbox,'
I say, putting the toy
onto the floor
and letting the teeth
clatter around,
'is from Ella
because she says
I talk too much!'

'You didn't tell them
what *I* gave you,'
Roxie grumbles.

But Miss Darling says,
'That's enough show and tell for today.
We have a busy morning ahead.'

Soon Roxie forgets to
frown and we all get excited about …

Vika.

Do-it-yourself

Vika is Miss Darling's friend
who's visiting from
the Solomon Islands.

In Vika's country,
kids don't have many toys,
and what they have,
Vika says,
they often make
themselves
from things in their
environment –
like sticks
and palm leaves,
or recycled tins and containers.

Not real toys
like our toys.

Home-made toys.

.

.

.

They must be
very clever kids to make
their own toys.

.

.

.

But I can't imagine
not getting *real* toys
for my birthday!

.

.

.

Tin Trucks

'Tin cans are precious,'
Vika says,
'because there aren't many –
and every kid in the village
wants one because
tins

      r … o … l … l

                  and make great

                        wheels.'

Imagine playing with a truck
made from an old powdered-milk tin
with a hole
through the centre
and a vine threaded through
dragging behind you
on a dusty track.

Or
that powdered-milk tin
rotating on the end of a
looooooong pole
that you can push
in front of you

along the dusty
track.

When Vika shows us photos
of kids playing with
their tin trucks,
I can almost hear
the shouts of laughter
and rattle of the cans
as they race along.

Then Vika shows pictures
of other toys kids have made
using things
they've found –
like twigs and berries,
sardine tins and bottle tops.

Some of them look like
real toy trucks!

I try to imagine constructing
a toy from
sticks, vines, berries
and other scraps
of found treasure

all held together
without any
glue …

But I can't.

Chop-chop!

Vika has brought
a helicopter
made from a hollow coconut shell,
some string
and a few pieces of wood.

'I can't see,' Heidi huffs.

'Everyone sit on your bottoms,' Miss Darling
   says –
        then waits …
                and waits …
                        until, *finally*,
                        even Jack
                        is sitting down
                        properly.

When Vika pulls the helicopter string,
the wooden blades whizz around – fast.

Jack's fingers are faster.

'Yee-ouch!' he cries,
as the wooden blades whack him
hard across the knuckles.

'What were you doing?'

    'I wanted to see how fast it was going.'

'I told everyone to sit down.'

    'I couldn't see.'

'You could have been hurt.'

    'I think it broke my fingers!'

'Go up to the office and get an icepack.'

    'I'm gonna make one of them at home.'

'That is *not* a good idea.'

Palm Snakes

Jack is back,
still talking about
the-helicopter-he's-going-to-make,
but Miss Darling says
we're doing something
a little simpler –
and a lot safer.

'Vika is going to show us
how to weave palm snakes.'

Jack groans.
'But I really want to know
how to make that helicopter!'

'If you don't listen,'
Miss Darling says,
'you won't know
what to do.'

Vika breaks off a leaf segment
from a fresh, green palm frond
and runs her fingernail
along the spine
so that, with a twist and pull,

she has two strips of green
joined at one end –
and one long, skinny twiggish-spine.

'At home,
we save the spines,'
Vika says,
doing sweeping movements
with her hands,
'to make a broom.'

Does that mean
they can't
buy a broom from
the shops?

Vika holds the end
where the
two green strips
join.

'This bit
sticking out
is the tongue,'
Vika says.

Then she concertina-folds the
strips,
over and over and over,
pinching them between her fingers
until they are bunched like a thick
bundle of pages.
Eventually the strips taper out ...
and are almost

gone.

'We need to leave enough
to tie a knot,' Vika says.

When Vika ties the tail
she releases her bundle of folds
and it springs out into a length
of criss-crossing green squares
almost like ...
                    a snake!

Michael the Bulldozer

It's fiddly making
palm snakes,
but it's also fun
talking with friends
and laughing each time
a thick bundle of coiled snake
springs out of our hands
and unravels on the floor.

Vika made it look so easy!

'Keep a good hold,' Vika says,
laughing and shaking her head
as she retrieves Kody's weaving.
'Here, try again.'

Michael says Kody's palm snake
looks like it's been run over
by a bulldozer.

It's true
that Kody's palm snake
has more bumps and bends
than Vika's,
but Kody was really trying hard …

until Michael tried to 'help'.

'Weaving's stupid,'
Kody says,
throwing his unfinished snake into the bin.
It uncoils into two crimped lengths
of palm leaf.

'I don't need to make a dumb snake,'
Kody sneers.
'Dad will buy me a real toy one
if I ask him.'

Rough and Tough

Vika helps me tie my snake's tail,
and I'm finished.

'You could make another
while you're waiting,'
Vika says.

Or maybe I could help someone else.

I run my palm snake through my hand
and feel the edges
gripping as it
rasps through.

I look around the room.

Miss Darling is helping Roxie.
        Vika is helping Heidi.
                Michael is *not* helping Ashton.

Kody is sprawled
in his chair –
arms crossed,
face creased –
staring
out the window.

I retrieve his weaving
from the rubbish,
and follow the crease lines,
folding so that soon it becomes
a snake again –
a bit lumpy-bumpy
and not very long,
but
a snake.

I walk across the room
and stop beside
Kody.

'You nearly finished this,'
I say quietly,
holding the snake out.
'It's the meanest palm snake
I've seen.'

(I've only ever seen Vika's palm snake,
and mine ...
but Kody doesn't seem to think about that.

And his snake *does* look rough and tough!)

Michael is too busy
'helping' Ashton
to notice Kody reach out
and take his snake
from me.

Kody doesn't say thank you.
He doesn't say anything.
But he doesn't throw
his snake away again,
or rip it into pieces
either.
He puts it on the desk in front of him,
his fingers pinching the ends together,
then turns
so his back
is a wall
in front of me.

I move away
to help Pia
tie the tail
on her snake.

When I look back,
Kody's tongue is twitching
on his bottom lip,
and that glumpy stub of snake
is slowly growing

l
o
n
g
e
r
.

What We Learnt

We are a flurry
of activity
(and noise),
tidying our room
after a
very busy morning.

When we're finished,
we sit on the carpet
and share
what we've learnt.

Roxie says she's learnt
how to weave a snake –
and now she wants to make
a basket or a mat
like she saw in Vika's pictures.

Jack says he
didn't learn how to make
a coconut helicopter …
but that doesn't mean he isn't
going to try and make one
at home.

Ashton says he learnt
that you can't escape from
housework,
even if you don't
have a broom!

Sara says
she's learnt
to be thankful
for all her toys.

I tell Miss Darling
that I'm glad
I don't live
in a country
where kids don't have
real toys.

Miss Darling smiles,
then asks if the kids
in Vika's photos
looked happy.

I think back to their
wide grins
and sparkling eyes
as they showed off their home-made toys
to the camera
like they were the most exciting things
they owned.

Maybe
making your own toys
is like
making art and craft.

Maybe I'd like it.

Maybe their one
home-made toy
means more to them
than *all* my toys
mean to me …

Maybe I Could

In the afternoon,
I tell Ella about
Vika's visit.
After we've done our homework,
we walk around the park
near our house
collecting
twigs and berries,
vines and leaves,
and all sorts of bits
that we can use
to make
toys.

'I want to make a boat,'
I tell Ella.
'But not just a looking-at one.
I want it to float.'

Ella
wants to make
a doll,
'with different outfits
she can wear:

a dress,
and pants,
and a shirt.'

'Dad can help us
if we get stuck,'
Ella says,
but I tell her
I want to do this

myself.

Float Your Boat

My boat
is very simple
and it's *just*
holding together –
but I didn't use
glue
(or staples
or sticky tape),
and I made it
all by
myself.

And it floats.

'It's not very good,'
I tell Miss Darling
the next morning,
as I push the twigs
back into the Styrofoam base,
'but it was fun to make.
And I like it.'

Miss Darling's eyes are shining
as she takes a photo

of me
holding my boat ...

grinning.

MAKING
FRIENDS

Helpers

During morning session,
Miss Darling asks me
to choose a friend
to help tidy the
classroom bookshelves
at first break.

I feel my smile
slide up my face
and crinkle into my eyes
as I stand tall
like a helium balloon
straining at the top
of a taut string.

My eyes scan
the kids in Year 2.
Nearly everyone
is looking right at me.

We all love helping
Miss Darling.

But not Kody
or Jack.

They wouldn't want
anything to interfere
with lunchtime cricket.

And not Lucy.
She sits head down,
eyes away.

I don't have any friends.

'Who are you going to choose?'
Roxie asks,
grabbing my hand
and squeezing my fingers.

'I wouldn't mind
missing out on playtime,'
she adds.

I see some of the
shoulders slump
around the classroom
as Roxie talks,
but others sit up straighter –
bodies leaning in,
eyes glued on
me.

Lucy
is tracing patterns
on the carpet.

I smile at Roxie,
hoping she will
understand,
then tell Miss Darling,

'I'd like Lucy to help me.'

My hand goes slack
as Roxie plops hard
onto the carpet
with a '*Humph*'.

Lucy's finger stills,
but she doesn't look up.

'Is that okay with you, Lucy?'
Miss Darling asks.

Lucy nods, slowly,
and Miss Darling
moves on to explain
our next task.

When everyone
is focused on Miss Darling,
Lucy's head lifts.
I see her eyes
slide quickly to me –
and just as quickly
away again.

I smile;
a small,
secret smile.

Roxie Forgets

Roxie
is in a huff
because I chose Lucy,
but then she remembers
that they haven't finished
their game in the rainforest,
and her huff is forgotten
as she spends
the eating break
organising everyone for
the game.

She doesn't even notice
when Lucy and I
disappear
into the classroom
at playtime.

Snail's Pace

Lucy is
quiet.

She works slowly
as we sort books
and arrange them on the shelves.
I chatter away,
telling her about
Ella, Mum and Dad,
and projects I'm making
at home using the special
craft materials
I got for my birthday.

Lucy nods.   Keeps working.

She listens and
doesn't say much
when I ask her questions
like:
      'How many people in your family?'
        'Me and Dad.'
      'Where's your mum?'
        Shrugs.

'Do you have any brothers or sisters?'

Shakes her head.

'Did you like your old school?'

'Which one?'

'How many have you been to?'

'I can't remember.'

'Why did you move?'

Looks away.

'Do you have any pets?'

'A snail.'

'What's its name?'

'Snail.'

'What does it look like?'

'A snail.'

She answers,
but her answers leave me
with *more* questions.

Why does Lucy move around so much?

Is that why she doesn't smile much?

Is she lonely?

What does she do with a pet snail?

(And why didn't she call it
        Shelly
                or Slime
                        or ... something?)

But I don't ask.

BREAKING
FRIENDS

Picture This

Now that our story is written
        (yippee!)
and edited
        (at last!),
Miss Darling says
it's time to talk about
illustrations
        (my favourite part!).

We have to work with a friend
to create a
plasticine collage illustration.

Miss Darling has ~~BIG~~

                    ~~enormous~~

                            stupendous plans!

'We're going to take photos
of your collages and
insert them into the story,'
Miss Darling says.
'Then we'll print and bind
a copy for everyone.'

'That's a lot of books!' Ashton says.

'Will there be a book for
Grandma and Grandad, too?'
Roxie asks.

'Can I have one for Mum
and one for Dad?'
Kody asks.

'I'm sure we'll be able to work something out,'
Miss Darling reassures us.

'Maybe Vika
can take some of our
books
back to the kids
in her village,'
I say.

'Oooh,
Miss Darling,
can she?'
Roxie asks
as excitement ripples around
the classroom.

'I'll have to talk
to Vika,'
Miss Darling says,
'but I think it's a
fantabulous idea.'

Art Partners

While Miss Darling has been talking,
my fingers have been
                    twitching
to push and mould
the plasticine
into pictures.

I can't wait to get started.

'Can I work with you, Tahnee?'
Pia asks,
as Heidi mouths,
'Me! Me! Me!'
her hands flourishing
around her face.

Then Roxie is there,
grabbing my arm
and dragging me closer.

'Tahnee's my partner.
I chose her first,
and we haven't worked together
in Art all year.'

'Can we work in a group of three?'
Pia asks Miss Darling.
'Or four?' I add.

Miss Darling shakes her head.

'There are 24 students in the class
and that's perfect for groups of two,'
she says.
'Why don't you and Heidi work together, Pia?
And Tahnee can work with Roxanne.'

'Maybe Heidi and Roxie can work together,'
I say, squeezing Roxie and Heidi's hands
so that they know we're still friends
and I'm not really NOT choosing them.

'I'm already working with Roxie
in our Technology group,
and I haven't worked with Pia
for a long time,' I say.

'Heidi, we can work together
next time.'

Pia's face opens like a sunflower
on a summer's day,
warming me with her happiness.

But Roxie is
as cold as an oyster shell
as she turns,
latching onto Heidi.
Head high,
shoulders stiff,
she doesn't look back
as she drags Heidi away.

Cold Lunch

At second break,
Pia and I are already eating
when Roxie and Heidi
arrive.

Heidi is smiling
as Pia and I wriggle over
to make room for them,
but Roxie grips Heidi's arm,
pulling her
                    away
                              from
                                        us.

'Let's sit by ourselves,'
Roxie says loudly,
'so we can talk about
our artwork.'

She sits
with her back towards us,
and tugs Heidi down
beside her,
near enough

that we can hear them,
but far enough
that they're not part of
our group.

Pia and I
talk quietly
and don't eat
or laugh much.

It's okay
that Roxie and Heidi
are sitting by themselves.

But the cold, stiff wall
that Roxie is building
between us
is not okay.

Dad Says

'It sounds like
you made a fair choice.'

'It's good to be friends
with everyone.'

'You can't be responsible
for Roxie's actions.'

'By tomorrow
she may have forgotten
all about it.'

'Just give her
some space.'

It's Not Over

On Wednesday
Roxie is sticking to Heidi
like a suction toy
in the bath.
But
I feel like I'm stuck
in an invisible glass wall,
as Roxie's eyes
            look
            right
            through
                me.

'Who's your best friend?'
Roxie asks Heidi
as they sit
together
at first break.

Heidi looks across
at me,
at Pia,
back at Roxie
and shrugs.

'You're all my friends,'
I hear her say.

And we are.

'But who's your *best* friend?'
Roxie pushes,
and Heidi looks at me,
away,
everywhere,
anywhere,
nowhere,
then drops her head
and whispers
something I
can't hear …

But Roxie does.

'I thought *I* was your best friend,'
Roxie sulks.
'Besides, Tahnee can't be
your best friend –
she's supposed to be
my best friend.'

Best Friends

I don't want to like
anyone best.
I just want to like
everyone!

Flat

At playtime,
Roxie
is like a basketball
that doesn't bounce.
And now
no-one wants to play
anymore.

Smile Wobbles

It's two days
since Roxie decided
I'm not her friend
(even though I am!),
and she is *still* not talking to me.

I try to smile
and be friendly,
but it's hard to look happy
when I'm hurting
inside.

Doesn't Roxie
like me
at all?

Friction Toys

Our group is *not*
working well
in Technology today.

Roxie
won't help;
she flicks specks of dirt
off the carpet
and doesn't even try
to be a part
of our group,
as she slumps forwards,
shoulders hunched,
hair hanging like a curtain

between

us.

Storming Brains

Even though
we're each going to
design
     and
         create
our own
recycled toy,
Miss Darling says,
'Work as a group
to brainstorm ideas
so you have
oodles of options
to choose from.'

Michael wants to make
a truck –
doesn't want to listen
to what
     anyone else
wants to make.

'That's stupid.'
  'Pffft!'
    'I'm not making that!'

'A truck's heaps better.'

'No-one said *you*
can't make a truck,'
Ashton tells him.
'But not everyone
wants to make
                    a *truck*.'

'What do you think, Roxie?' I ask.
'You always have good ideas.'

But Roxie
doesn't look,
doesn't answer –
drops her shoulder
so I'm faced
with
        her back.

'Miss Darling says to write down
all ideas,'
Sara says,
'so we can choose the
best ideas.'

'A truck *is* the best idea.'

Michael scowls, as Sara writes

- truck
  (Michael)
  - doll
    (Sara)
- windmill-pinwheel
  (Tahnee)
  - cricket bat
    (Ashton)
  - pull-along
    animal toy
    (Sara)

- a cup-and-ball
  catcher thing
  joined by string
  (Tahnee)
  - boat
    (Ashton)
  - a marble
    racer
    (Ashton)
    - ???
      (Roxie)

'I'm still doing a truck,' Michael says.

'We know!' Ashton, Sara and I chorus.

Roxie just huffs.

Kept In

At the end of the day Miss Darling
lets us go one by one until
the only one on
the carpet is
me.

'Has something happened
      between you
        and Roxanne?'
Miss Darling asks,
as kids jostle and jest
outside the classroom.

My teacher's eyes
are want-to-help-you warm,
and she waits
as I think about
what to say.

'Roxie's upset,'
I tell Miss Darling,
'because I didn't
choose her
to be my Art partner.

She thinks
we aren't friends
now …'

'And what do you think?'
Miss Darling asks.

'I think …
it's hard to be a friend
when Roxie won't listen
anymore.'

An Idea

Miss Darling
thinks Roxie is sad and
sorry, and maybe she doesn't
know how to make things right.
I think Roxie is also awkward-
embarrassed and just can't
do it by herself. But I
have an idea. Maybe
it will help fix
things. I hope
so because I
miss Roxie.

MYSTERY MESSAGES

Note to Self

When I get home from school
I tell Dad about
my idea.

He thinks it's a *great* idea.

'Come and see me if you get stuck,'
Dad says,
as he starts clearing up
our afternoon-tea things.

I smile.

It's good to know
Dad's there –
but I have things
I need to say.

I gather coloured paper
from my craft table
and my brightest felt pens.

Then I start
to write.

You are a good friend
because you are always
kind.   (Pia)

You are a good friend
because you treat others
with respect.   (Heidi)

You are a good friend
because you make me laugh.   (Ashton)

You are a good friend
because you encourage others.   (Sara)

All afternoon,
I work on my messages.
Some are easier
than others.

You are a good friend
because
you help everyone
get organised.   (Michael)

You are a good friend
because
you listen
lots!   (Lucy)

You are a good friend
because
you don't quit
even if you think
your dad could do it
better.   (Kody)

By tea time,
I've written
22 messages
for the friends in my class –

You are a good teacher because
you smile lots
and make
school
FUN!

– and one for Miss Darling.

But there is one more message
that I still need to write.

And I don't know what to say.

I have so many friends.

  But I miss Roxie.

What can I write
to make things
better?

Secret Squirrel

After tea,
Mum and Dad
read my messages.

Sometimes they help me
fix little things –
but mostly they smile
and nod their heads,
and sometimes sniff a little
and wipe their eyes.

'You are such a good friend,'
Mum says,
'because you care
about *every*one.'

'Tahnee,
are all your friends
really this good?'
Ella asks,
her eyebrows raised
in disbelief.
'Like Michael …
and Kody … and …'

I start to laugh.

'Not all the time, silly.
        But they can be.'

I start slipping the notes
into their
labelled,
decorated
envelopes,
then stack them
on my desk
in alphabetical order.

'Do you think anyone will know
who wrote them?'
Ella asks.

I pause, thinking.

'I'm not telling anyone
(not even Miss Darling),
but I think
        Roxie
will guess.

She always knows
when it's
me.'

Forever Friends

You are a good friend because
you have been my friend
forever
and I like being
with you.   (Roxie)

Hide-and-seek

Dad drops us at school
early
so that I can
begin to hide
the secret messages
for my friends
to find.
I hide them
in all sorts of
places.

Secret Admirer

'*Woooo woooo*,'
Jack cries,
as Michael opens his
tidy tray and finds
the letter
on top.

'Michael's got a girlfriend,'
Jack chirps
in a singsong voice.

Michael goes red
and fumbles the envelope
so it flutters to the floor
as Jack hoots and howls,
and Miss Darling
claps her hands
three times,

then waits …

'Bring the envelope to me,'
she says.

Puzzling

When the class is settled
and busy with a
handwriting activity,
Miss Darling talks quietly
to Jack
and Michael.

I try not to look,
but I want to see
what happens;
I don't want to get
my friends in trouble.

Miss Darling talks
to Jack,
who doesn't look
quite so cheeky
when he walks
back to his seat.

Michael opens
the note
and reads,

then shrugs
before passing it
to Miss Darling.

At first
Miss Darling
seems puzzled,
but then her face brightens
as she slips the note back into
the envelope
and passes it to Michael.

'I think someone is just
being a good friend
and encouraging you,'
Miss Darling says.
'What a great idea.'

My heart is jazz dancing
as I put my head down
and focus on
my handwriting.

Not So Woooo Woooo

Jack doesn't
say anything more about
girlfriends,
especially when he finds
a note in *his* Maths book.

'Are you sure
you didn't write this, Miss?
You are a good friend
because you make us LOL
doing
        unexpected
things.'

Miss Darling's eyes sparkle.
'Well, you do make me laugh—'

Jack splutters,
but he's goofy-grinning as
Miss Darling continues,

'—but I didn't write it.

            I wonder who did?'

You're a Good Friend

All through the morning,
I see my friends'
faces light up
as they discover
and read
their messages.

Miss Darling is puzzled
…
but pleased.

'I don't know who's responsible,'
she says,
'but I like it.'

I like it, too!

Lucy's Letter

When Lucy
opens her note
at first break,
I see her eyebrows
furrow in concern,
then relax
as a small smile creeps across
her face.

If I wasn't watching closely
I might have missed it.

But it's there –

the slightest tilt
to her lips.

'Want to come to the library?'
I ask Lucy, when the play bell rings.

'We could read a book
or do some drawing,
or even …

talk.'

Lucy looks at me –
looks really closely –
then nods.

And her tiny smile
is just that teensy tiniest bit
bigger.

'Okay,' she says.

What if Roxie ...

I wish I knew
what Roxie did
when she found
her note.
But I didn't see,
and I don't even know
if she read it –
if she *found* it.

I put her envelope
in the rainforest,
wedged into the V of
our favourite tree.

But what if she didn't go there?

What if the Year 3 boys
found it first?

What if Roxie thinks
she's the only one
who didn't get
a message?

What if she knows I wrote
the notes and thinks
I skipped her
on purpose?

What was I thinking
when I put
Roxie's letter
in such a special,
silly
place?

I wanted to make things better –

not worse.

THE
SECRET
TO
FRIENDS

For Me?

During afternoon session,
I open my desk

and ...

What a shock!

There's an envelope
in my tidy tray,
with *my* name on it.

I didn't write me a message.

How did it get there?

I glance around the room,
but no-one is watching.

There's sticky tape
holding the envelope together,
as though someone
made it.

On the flap
there's a drawing
of two girls:
one has yellow-blonde hair,

one has red hair.

I lift the flap and
draw out
the message
written on yellow paper;
my favourite colour.

> You are a good friend
> because you care about
> everyone,
>
> and
> I miss
> you.

This time
I look straight up
at Roxie.
She's watching me,
a smile
testing her lips,
questioning her eyes.

I wave the note
at Roxie
and giggle

as she starts crazy mimes
of happiness.

Miss Darling is watching
with a frown on her face,
but I point
to Roxie and the letter
as I grin
all the way down
to my toes …

Miss Darling softens.

'It's silent reading time,
girls,' she says,
holding her finger to her lips.

But she's smiling, too.

Best of Secrets

Even though
Roxie knows
who wrote the
notes,
she isn't telling anyone,
and I don't think
it matters anymore
because, on Monday,
our classroom
is like
a good-friends
post office.

Everyone is sending
messages.

> You are a good friend
> because you like me
> just the way
> I am.

You are a good friend
because you are funny.

You are a good friend
because you play fair
at cricket.

You are a good friend
because you help me.

You are a good friend
because you are my friend
even when
I make mistakes.

You are a good friend
because you are
a good friend.

Snap!

After we've
marked the roll,
Miss Darling
scans the class,
her eyes bright.

'I spoke to Vika
about your story
                idea.
She said the kids
in her village
would love your storybooks
and she will *make* room
for them in her suitcase.'

Everyone
claps
and cheers.

Miss Darling makes
hushing hands
and our voices quieten
to a burble.

'I wish we could
be there
when they see
our books,'
Ashton says.

I remember Vika's photographs –
grinning kids holding home-made
toys.

'Maybe Vika will take a photo,' I say.

'And send it to us,' Roxie cries.

'Maybe she will, but—'
Miss Darling projects our story onto
the whiteboard,
'—we need to finish the books first!'

What's the Plan?

During middle session,
we start planning
and designing
our recycled
push-pull toys.

'What are you
going to do, Roxie?'
I ask.

Roxie looks at our
brainstorming sheet
and sneaks a cheeky grin.

'I'm not going to make
a truck!' she whispers,
and we giggle –
                 quietly.
We do NOT want to hear
any more about
trucks!

'I
wanted to
weave   a basket,' Roxie says, 'like in
Vika's   pictures … But Mum helped me look
on the internet, and that seems too tricky. Then
I found a fish you can weave, using palm leaves,
so I'm   going to make enough for a
mobile   full of flying, palm-leaf
fish.'

Frog-and-fly Catcher

What are you making,
Tahnee?' Sara asks.

'I'm going to make
a toilet-roll frog
with a long, red string tongue
attached to a cork fly,'
I tell her.
'You hold the frog
like a cup,
then flick it
and try to catch
the fly.'

'Wow. That's really cool,'
Ashton says.

Michael frowns.
'Well, I'm still going to make—'

I look at Roxie, Ashton and Sara,
and we all
make loopy, laughing faces
as we finish Michael's sentence,

'—a truck!'

Friends Shared

At second break
I choose a different place
      to sit.

Heidi, Pia and Roxie
start walking
to our normal seat –
then stop,
look around
and finally
                see me
waving at them
from my place
on the concrete
with Lucy.

I point
to all the space
beside us,
then grin
      and beckon them over.

Roxie looks at
our usual seat,
    then at Pia and
        Heidi,
            then at Lucy
                and me (holding my breath).

Then,
chattering like magpies,
they swoop
            towards us.

Sharing Ideas

Lucy keeps eating –
doesn't react
when Roxie, Heidi and Pia
sit down
and start   unclipping,
                    unzipping,
          unwrapping
their lunches.

'What are you all making
for your
recycled toy project?'
I ask,
as everyone
settles.

Pia
says she's making
a musical instrument
with shells and buttons
inside a plastic bottle;

she says it will look
and sound
pretty
as it rolls and rattles
along.

Heidi is making
a bird –
a budgie –
a blue one,
using a toilet roll
and fabric
and a piece of string
to swing
and make it fly.

'It won't be the same
as Bluey,'
Heidi says.
'I still miss him.'

Roxie tells us about
her palm-leaf fish mobile.

'It sounds tricky,' says Pia.

I look at Lucy
focused on
trailing her finger
around an imaginary spiralling circle
on the concrete
in front of her.

'And you, Lucy?' I ask.

Lucy's finger slows its trail
as she peers cautiously
at me.

> 'What are you making?'
>   'A snail.'
> 'What sort of snail?'
>   'A toy one.'

A Trail of Questions

Ever so
snail-slowly,
we start to unravel
Lucy's plan.

'So, two large plastic lids
are the snail shell?'
Pia asks,
as Lucy nods.

'And the paper-towel roll
goes between the lids
to be the body,'
Heidi says.

'And the head,' Lucy adds,
'with eyes.'

'And a skewer will join
the shell and the body,' I say,
'but the skewer will let
the shell roll—'

              '—like wheels!' Roxie finishes.

Lucy is nodding,
her eyes bright
as they flick from
face to face.

'A snail pull-toy is clever, Lucy,'
Pia says,
and we all agree.

'It's perfect for you!' I tell Lucy.

The play bell rings,
and we start to gather up
our lunch gear.

'I can't wait to see
all our toys,' I say.
'They're

      so …

           different!

Snail Mail

On Tuesday
when I arrive at school,
the classroom
is quiet
   and empty.
A crumpled envelope
sits on my desk.
Someone has crossed out
the typed address
and written
      Tarny
in blue pen.

      Curious,
        I open
      the envelope
      and pull out
            a flyer for pizza.

Is someone playing
   a joke on me?

I turn it over
and notice writing
   in the same blue pen.
      Words
            spiral
               out from the
            centre
         of the page
      like …

a snail!

Carefully
twirling the paper
around I read:

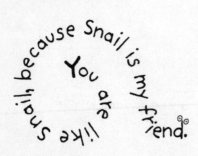

My tummy
flips cartwheels
as I slide the message

back into the envelope
and tuck it safely
into my tidy tray.

Then I skip out to
the playground
looking for
my friends.

'Tahnee!
You're here.'

'What are you
going to play, Tahnee?'

> 'Tahnee,
> come to the library
> with us!'

>> 'Do you want to
>> skip with us,
>> Tahnee?'

>>> 'Let's play
>>> horses today!'

I look
around
the bustling playground
of friends
and spot Lucy
standing,

       watching.

       'Come and play!'
     I say,

         smiling.

Acknowledgements

To Karyn, who told me of a little girl who had too many friends, sparking a story that has been pure joy to write; to Kristina and Kristy, who heard the heart in the story, and helped me hunt the missing beats, and to Jo, whose illustrations are my works of heart; to the chain of paper dolls who have enlivened my classrooms – the serious and the mischievous, the hurting and the caring – each oh-so-wonderfully unique; to the passionate educators who pour their heart into inspiring and uplifting kids to be their best; to my jumbo pack of assorted party lollies who encourage and enrich with their own flavour of friendship; and to my family, who don't sugar-coat their words, but are the sweet treats in my life; in so many ways, you have all contributed to this book, and I thank you.

BULLY ON THE BUS
Kathryn Apel

Winner Australian Family Therapists' Award
for Children's Literature: Young Readers

She's big.
    She's smart.
        She's mean.

She picks on me and
I don't know how to make her stop.

Leroy has a 'Secret Weapon', but will it help him find the strength and courage he needs to overcome the bully's taunts once and for all?

A beautifully crafted verse novel that will surprise and inspire you, and warm your heart.

'An important book as well as a brilliantly creative one. Highly recommended.'
Kids' Book Review

'A lovely story and a great way to tackle bullying.'
Herald Sun

ISBN 978 0 7022 5328 7